Heavy Metal Lust

Victoria Blisse

Love,
Victoria Blisse
x

Victoria Blisse

Heavy Metal Lust

CHAPTER ONE

The racket vibrates through every fibre of me. The sea of bodies all around me roll with joy in time to the beat. Head thrashing, toe-tapping, whole body jumping masses of delight, mostly teenaged, it has to be said.

My ears hurt. I'm too old for this shit.

I wait patiently for the screaming, thumping, reverberating aural assault to stop, tap my daughter's shoulder and wait for her to make eye contact before leaning in to yell in her ear over the screaming around us.

"I'm nipping out for a bit. Will you be okay?"

"Yeah, sure. You not enjoying Eyebleed?" She grins widely.

"No, no I'm not. I'll be back when they've finished. Message me if you need me."

"Yes, Mum." A new song starts and Amy starts screaming and bouncing up and down till the metal on her boots clanks and her long, dyed black fringe covers her face. I scurry between bodies until I reach the edge of the auditorium where I stride confidently and quickly to the foyer within the first few bars of the next song.

I'm outside before the band starts to make noise. There's no way that sound could ever be described as singing. Really, I'm not that uncool—the main band, Black Tranquillity, are actually quite good. But this screaming stuff does not appeal to my music taste. It's barely music.

The big doors to the 1930s theatre turned 70s music venue are still open so I can hear more than I really want of the noise. I wander round the side of the hulking grey building hoping to seek silence, well if not silence an organic low hum that, no doubt, will be replicated in my bed tonight after the assault on my ears.

The things we do for the love of a thirteen year old offspring. She doesn't ask for much–okay, she asks for a lot, but generally accepts a no with good grace—and so I give in and let her go to these concerts once in a while. Even though my ear health plummets with every one.

It's worth it, though, to see and feel her excitement. As a single mum I'm always worried that she's not getting all a girl her age should. Not enough of my time because I have to work, not enough treats because the money I work for is peanuts, and not enough opportunity to just be a kid because she has grown up quickly. She's had to be there for me, too.

There's not much of a view to admire here, but I'm looking out over the area of scrubland and car park while I walk and so it comes as quite a surprise when the toe of my shoe impacts something very solid and I stumble. It's even more surprising when hands reach out to steady me.

"Oh, I'm sorry," I stutter, gawping at the guy who is steadying me, "I wasn't looking where I was going."

"No, no, my fault entirely. Should keep my big size tens tucked away. Are you okay?"

"Yeah, fine, thank you." He has stunning eyes. A swirling green patchwork that mesmerises me. His lips are pretty too, plump and ripe and—*snap out of it woman*—he's very young.

"You sure?" He squeezes my shoulder. I nod far too hard and for far too long. His touch is hot and when he removes his hand I can still feel the imprint of his fingers.

Really, I should be moving on, not standing and gawking at him. A black beanie hides the majority of his hair, excerpt for a few dark strands that peek out around his ears. An oversized black hoodie—probably sporting a band logo on the back—masks what might be under there, but the skinny jeans don't leave a thing to the imagination.

"Would you like a cig?" He pulls a dog eared packet from his back pocket.

"Nah, I've not smoked in years."

"Yeah, I'm trying to give up. Hard work, though. Especially with the guys smoking around me all the time."

"That's really difficult. Only time I crave it now is when I'm in a group of smokers. My lungs are happier now, though."

“So, why you out here then? Not enjoying the band?”

I wonder if he’s deliberately trying to keep me talking or if he’s just a naturally chatty person, so I reply without much thought. “God no, it’s horrific noise. All screamy and bangy and urgh.” I shake my head. “My daughter really loves it all. That’s why I’m here.”

“Ah, not a fan then?” His smile is curiously quizzical.

“Not of Eyebleed, no. Black Tranquillity are pretty good, mind. I can sing along to their stuff and their lead singer is pretty easy on the eye. I’ll head in for that. I’ll embarrass my daughter by old woman bopping along to the tunes, can’t miss out on that.”

“Oh, hush. You’re not old!” He exclaims.

“Why, thanks, but I’m old enough to be your mother.” I chuckle, cheeks warming.

“Pfft.” He shakes his head. “Well, however old you are, you’re gorgeous.”

Now, I’m a wordy person. I work in advertising, I spend most of my working week speaking and hardly ever shut up in my own time either. There isn’t a single thing I can say. Not a thought in my brain to push out onto my lips. I’m completely taken aback.

I look at him, then at the ground, then back at him. His green eyes are rimmed with hazel brown and his pupils are huge. I gulp, giggle, and look again to the floor.

Eloquent.

"And wonderfully cute too."

"Oh!" I finally manage to squeak out a response. "Stop it."

"What if I don't want to?"

"Then, well... I guess I'll have to do something to stop you!"

"Oh, yes?" He grins widely. If this was a cartoon, devil horns would grow out of his forehead. "Well, I have to say I've not been able to take my eyes off you because I just can't believe how beautiful you are. There's your amazing eyes–deep and dark—and your hair, so sleek and smooth I just want to reach out and run my fingers through it–"

"I can't see your hair 'cos of the beanie so I don't know if I want to touch it."

I talk shit when I'm panicking.

"Oh, I'll take it off for you then." He chuckles, tipping his head forward and pulling the hat off. His hair is soft and dark, long on top and shaved at the side. It's when he flicks the long strands across his face that I see something that makes my jaw drop.

A lightning bolt.

"Thunder?" I gasp. "You're Thunder—oh shit."

He laughs. "You really didn't realise?"

I hadn't, not at all. Which, considering he's plastered all over my daughter's room, is pretty telling of my observational skills.

I just shake my head. Once again completely lost for words and this time wishing a rogue wind would whip me up and fly me away from the embarrassment.

"Ha, I thought you were just being coy with the lead singer comment."

"Oh hell, I said you were –I—oh dear."

"Look, erm, what's your name?"

"Josephine. Jo, I'm Jo."

"Okay, Josie." Again, that quirky little smile that shouts mischief flickers across his face. "I have to go because I'm on stage in like, ten minutes, but here's my number..." He pulls out a pen and rips the front off his cigarette packet.

"Give me a ring after the concert and we can go for a drink."

"Oh, that's lovely. I mean, I would, but my daughter... I have to get her home."

"Oh, yeah of course. You know, we're here tomorrow night too. Come along to the gig. I won't tell if you come in after Eyebleed finish." He winks and elbows me gently, making me blush even more. "And we can get together after it's all finished then, yeah?"

"Well, possibly. Maybe. I'd like to."

"Okay, cool." He presses the cardboard into my hand and kisses my cheek. "See you tomorrow, Josie."

He pulls his beanie on and strolls to the back of the theatre, knocks on a door and is virtually dragged in by a muscly arm. He waves just before he disappears and I wave back. My hand remains in the air even when he's completely gone from sight.

My phone beeps and pulls me out of my daze. It's Amy, wondering if I've got lost. I reply that I'm on my way and return to the concert with my mind whirling.

Amy isn't really interested in me once I get back to her, as soon as she knows I'm safe her focus goes to the stage dressings. The distinctive Black Tranquillity logo on a huge banner, instruments with flames and lightning bolts on them, and for some reason only a rock band might understand, a rusty old cage in the corner.

And just when I think I might blurt out that I'd met Thunder Jackson, the house lights dim, the music screams and the crowd roars and surges forward towards the guy I'd just been chatting to. He stands in the spotlight, microphone poised, body relaxed, gaze to the ceiling.

When the music starts there's no hope of me communicating anything to Amy, or anyone at all, in fact. All eyes are on the stage, including mine. It's strange. The man up there looks so different to the guy I was just chatting to but also completely and utterly the same. He has the same lazy sexuality, his movements fluid and rhythmic. He dances to the music without effort, or so it seems, and every now and then he gazes out into the crowd, causing a wave of hysteria.

There's no way that gorgeous, statuesque icon had been hitting on me. But the piece of cigarette packet in my jeans pocket says something completely different.

At every concert there's a moment where a lusting fan is looked at from the stage by the object of their desire. Everyone knows it's an illusion. But just when I'm contemplating ripping up his number and throwing it in the bin, avoiding any more embarrassment and shame, he looks at me.

Those green, swirling eyes, the pouting smile, all focused on me, making me believe that there could be something between us. When he looks away I'm released from the spell and realise everyone around me is thinking the same thing, but I can't let go of the dream.

***

We stay for the encore, of course, then follow the other, loudly exclaiming audience members into the cool night air. We discuss our favourite moments–I say we, what I mean is Amy tells me hers—and dance between the hawkers to get to the bus stop.

"So, why were you outside so long? I was worried," Amy slots in seamlessly.

"Oh, yeah. Well—" I can't tell my daughter a lie. "I was talking to a guy." I blush and duck my head, just like a teen talking about their crush.

"Really? Oh my God, did you get his number?" Amy squeals.

"Yeah, I did. He wants to take me out tomorrow night but—"

"No buts, Mum, you're going. What've I been telling you for months? You need a man in your life."

"But you'll be in school tomorrow and I can't leave you home alone."

"I'll stay at Kirsty's." She shrugs. "We've got science homework we need to do anyway so we can do that, then I can stay over there."

"I'd have to ring her mum, and it is short notice." I hiss through my teeth. A noise I never thought I'd make, but a regular one in my wheelhouse since becoming a mum.

"Stop making excuses. Ring Kirsty's mum in the morning. It'll be fine. You *have* to go on this date."

"God, Amy, you make me sound desperate."

"Well, you are," she says with the blunt disregard of a girl with many years left to live. "You haven't had a date since I was like, six."

"You were seven, actually," I correct her. "And I've been concentrating on other more important things. Like bringing you up. "

"Oh, rubbish. You're just scared. Nigel's dad—you know Nigel, he's in my French lesson—well, his dad was just like you, a total recluse. Nigel got him an account on Date a Dad about six months ago and now he's engaged!"

"Anyone would think you wanted rid of me," I grumble, shuffling onto the bus, sardined amongst other happy, loud and sweaty concertgoers.

"No, I just want to see you happy, Mum. You spend way too much of your time at work or looking after me."

"That's called being a mum." I smile, squeezing the top of her arm. "I love it."

"I'm sure you do. But you need more in your life, Mum. You're old before your time."

"Says you," I scoff. "Thirteen going on forty."

She rolls her eyes.

"Fine, fine. I'll ring Claire in the morning and see if it's okay for you to stay over. You bullied me into it."

She's just given me the excuse I need to actually go for it. God, what would Thunder think of that? I needed my daughter to goad me into actually going out with him. Well, meeting him at least. I still can't believe this is happening to me.

As I'm getting ready for bed, I pull the ratty piece of packet out of my pocket. It takes a few moments to input the numbers and save them into my phone and a lot longer to think about what to write in my text to him.

Will take you up on your offer for tomorrow night. Lovely chatting to you. Josie x

I've never thought of myself as a Josie, but that's what he called me and I need all the help I can get in making sure he knows who's texting him.

***

I stare at the ceiling, sleep evading me. My ears are humming and my brain is racing. What if he didn't mean it? What if he was pissed or stoned and he didn't know what he was doing? What if he was joking? Maybe I shouldn't go at all. I'll only make a fool of myself when I find my name not on the guest list.

The buzzing of my phone startles me. I pick it up, I go to just turn off the sound. Everyone knows these days that screen time with all that blue light stops you sleeping. I'm forever telling Amy off for it. So I very quickly turn it on and slide the sound off, checking that I have set the alarm. But I notice the notification on my lock screen. It's from Thunder.

Awesome. I want to get to know the sexy Josie all the more. You'll be on the guest list with a VIP pass.

Jump in the priority queue when you get there. I'll see you after the show. Can't wait. Thunder x

Firstly I'm relieved by the complete lack of text speak—I can't take that seriously. But then the relief spreads because I realise he does want to see me again. Me. Old enough to be his mother, me. For the first time in many years I fall asleep with a smile on my lips and butterflies in my stomach. A grand adventure awaits.

CHAPTER TWO

I'm an adult. I'm grown up. I'm in control. I can do this.

Walking up to the front of the Apollo Theatre is a completely different experience tonight. Yesterday I had Amy gabbing in my ear and it was her who was excited and giddy. Tonight I feel like a teenager. There are a million different thoughts running through my brain and I don't know how to keep up with them all. I'm usually in control. I make sure of it in fact. Being the responsible adult in a relationship, the one who has to make the money, who has to keep the home tidy, who has to look after the other one, nurture and encourage her until she is old enough to look after herself has drained all the reckless irresponsibility out of me. I'm reliable and a font of common sense on a day to day basis.

This is just sheer craziness.

There was a time when I was carefree and the only important thing in my life was that I was having fun. That ended quite abruptly when my mum got diagnosed with cancer and I became her sole carer. It was while I cared for her I met a guy, fell in love and had Amy. I settled down—the problem was Carl wasn't ready to settle down with me.

Fun became the last thing on my mind as I looked after my mum through her last days and brought up my little girl through her first. I always imagined there'd be time, somewhere down the line, for fun again, but responsibility has to take priority and feeding, clothing and housing a grown woman and her teen daughter isn't cheap. It's amazingly time consuming too.

God bless Claire for taking Amy at such short notice. She didn't seem at all fazed—in fact she was as excited as my daughter that I was finally going on a date. I'm glad they're happy about it. Me? I'm not even sure this is a date. I mean, Thunder is a metal star with a rock 'n' roll reputation. He's not looking to date me—if anything, he'll just want to fuck me.

Honestly, I wouldn't say no. He's hot and I haven't had sex in a very, very long time. Well, not with anyone other than myself or my trusty vibe. Even solo sex is ridiculously infrequent. Me time just doesn't happen very often.

Part of me is ready to turn around, go and pick up a pizza to eat naked in front of the telly, then take myself and my vibrating friend to bed. I might have turned around if I hadn't been asked for my ticket by a very gruff security guard.

"I'm on the guest list. Erm, Josie."

He looks, nods, and directs me inside, to the left of a rope divider. I'm given a lanyard with a VIP pass on it.

"After the show if you come back to this entrance you'll be able to get backstage. Don't go to the front of the stage, that's just for the groupies," the smiling host in a bright red jacket tells me. I imagine I look new to this and as nervous as I feel.

"Oh, okay, thank you." I nod.

"Enjoy the show. Erm, you might need earplugs, honey. It gets loud."

It's not until I get out into the auditorium and find myself a relatively quiet corner at the back that I realise how judgemental the host was being. She clearly hadn't seen me here last night. I know how loud it gets but I don't have earplugs. I actually kinda like the noise.

As the affront wears off I wonder if I've picked an appropriate outfit. I've gone for something approaching sexy. It's not a staple in my usual professional or comfortable wardrobe so it was a hard job finding anything at all. But tucked up in the corner of the wardrobe I found a little red dress I have never worn. When I first bought it in the sales, I loved the colour and the cut of the skirt but I hadn't realised how much boob it showed until I tried it on at home.

And that was before Amy had told me I was not allowed to go out wearing *that*. Good job she wasn't around tonight to see me leaving the house with it on. She'd turn beetroot red in mortification. Which to be fair, is probably a good indication that the dress is in fact, sexy. Possibly, though, not very metal concert appropriate. Even teamed with my trusty denim jacket and knee high boots. Anyway, it's too late to change my mind now. I'm here, I'm in, and apparently I've got a date with Thunder.

And it turns out that's his real name. I did a bit of Googling and I couldn't find any details on a real name at all. So either his mother was a bit of a hippy or he changed it by deed poll. It leads me to wonder what kind of man is called Thunder.

I should probably ask my daughter, since she knows everything anyone needs to know about Black Tranquillity, but she'd only wonder why I was suddenly so interested and she'd not believe me anyway if I told her. I'm not sure *I* believe me and I'm here, watching the same show I watched last night, but this time I'm really paying attention.

He does look good on stage, like he's at home there. He dances around, the individual movements thrashing and erratic but with a flow that is natural and beautiful in its way. He commands the whole audience, sure to look in all directions as he performs. He times everything perfectly. The cheeky tongue pokes and the statuesque stances that get the crowd roaring with pleasure and screaming his name.

I can see he's loving every moment of it, too—he feeds off the waves of adoration that roll over him.

I'm sure if you ask every lovesick boy and girl in the place to tell you their favourite moment they'd all say the same thing...ish.

'That moment when Thunder looked right at me.'

I'm not a naive youngster, I know it's just a deception of my mind or the light or a very clever trick. After all, it happened last night. But while he sings *Restless Beast*, my favourite of Black Tranquillity's songs, he looks right at me. Right into me, in fact. Like he did last night. I'm undone, exposed and emotional, like any of the kids in the place.

I realise why I'm here. I'm here just in case the dream can come true, that I, the plainest of Janes, can seduce a rock star. In his gaze, I believe I can do it, I'm emboldened by the magic of the moment. But when the song ends, reality seeps back in and I start to doubt myself again.

I'm vibrating with nerves after the final encore as the auditorium empties. I have to make my way to the VIP entrance, but I'm stuck to the floor. Only part of that is physical, however. What do they spill to make the floor so damn sticky, anyway?

There is a lot to be said for being a coward. It saves you from embarrassment and pain and preserves the status quo. The idea of just leaving, walking out and going home without any need for confrontation and/or possible disappointment is a very attractive one.

Damn the strength of my guilty conscience, though, because I've not even taken a step towards the exit before I'm worrying about what Thunder will think of me, leading him on, taking his generous offer, and then just leaving without even thanking him.

Bloody British manners, bred into me by my ever-so-proper mother.

It's not too anxiety-inducing getting backstage. I follow the gaggle of giggling groupies in front of me into a relatively small room with a few sofas and a table with snacks and small fridges full of cans.

While the groupies home in on the freebies, I sit in the corner of one of the well worn brown leather sofas and avoid looking at the teenagers scavenging for alcohol and snacks. It's worrying to think that could well be Amy soon enough.

When the girls sit down, gabbing and laughing and studiously ignoring me, I feel very much like the unwanted chaperone, and when they start throwing crisps at each other I really want to yell at them to behave and stop making a mess. It's really hard to turn the mummy habits off even when my kid isn't in tow.

There is nothing quite as ear piercing as an excited teenager's squeal. I look up when the girls go ultrasonic and leap from their seats. I think I catch a glimpse of Thunder before he's engulfed by the gabbling hoard.

I didn't anticipate needing to fight my way through a sea of rampaging super-fans to get to him. I don't know quite what I was expecting, but watching him being mauled by pretty young girls isn't really doing it for me and I'm not going to fight them for his attention.

Standing, I head past the loud, pawing mass towards the door.

"Josie! Hey, wait."

Thunder extracts himself from the centre of the swirling, twittering crowd with relative ease. The wide as they are tall security guards watch on, poised and ready for action if needed, but the girls shift their attention to the other band members with only a few dagger-like looks thrown my way.

"It's good to see you." He grins, opening his arms.

"And you." I step forward, giving him unspoken permission to wrap me in an embrace. It's a little surreal, especially now I'm aware of who he is. The guy who adorns posters in my teen's bedroom is hugging me, tightly.

He smells of sea salt and limes. I imagine he's just had a shower, since he was sweating up a storm on stage not so long ago. His stubble scrapes my skin as he presses his lips to my cheek. They're plump and soft, and even that gentle, polite kiss sends hot excitement streaming through my veins.

"Did you enjoy the gig?" He pulls back but leaves one hand on the top of my right arm.

"Yeah, thanks, I did." I nod enthusiastically. "Did you?" I shake my head. "Sorry, that was a daft question."

“No, no, it isn’t. I did enjoy it tonight, thanks. Sometimes it’s like the crowd and the band are one entity feeding off each other’s energy, and other nights you feel like you’re playing to a room full of dolls. Tonight was electric.”

“I thought it looked like you were enjoying yourself, but then that could just be some kind of clever performer skill, I don’t know.”

“Oh, you can learn how to play a crowd, how to fill the stage, but you can’t fake the kind of connection we had tonight—and last night actually. It’s been a good couple of gigs.”

“Excellent.” I nod, letting my smile grow.

“Mostly because of you and that smile.”

“Oh.” I feel the heat of the blush rising over my cheeks. “That’s kind of you to say.”

“Look, I need to sign some shit for these kids—it’s a contest thing—but I won’t be long. We can go for a drink or something then, yeah?” He squeezes my arm then lets go.

“Okay, I’d like that.”

“Take a seat. I’ll be done in a minute.”

I watch from the safe corner of the sofa while the band fend off the flighty girls. Autographs and selfies, raised voices and laughter—the guys patiently take it all before the hassled security guards round up the teens and herd them out into the corridor.

"Thank fuck for that," the one I think is called Grant, says on a sigh. He's the drummer, if I've got it right.

"Let's not do any more of those stupid meet the band contests," echoes the bassist, whose name escapes me completely. "We always end up surrounded by teenyboppers. I can be doing without that after a long, hard gig."

"Well, you fuckers can sit here and piss and moan. I'm going out with the lovely Josie tonight. Don't wait up."

Thunder grabs my hand and pulls me up off the sofa.

"Watch that one, Jos," Grant yells, "he's a bad boy."

"Don't believe everything you read, Reedsy. You're only jealous 'cos they paint you as the boring goody-two-shoes, anyway."

I don't need the warning. I know Thunder's reputation. Even outside the metal world, people know of it. There are quite often photos of him in the celeb magazines, arm around some woman—or several—accompanied by stories of benders and orgies and all sorts of depraved stuff. But I never believe what I read in the press—most of it's just made up anyway.

"It's okay—I'm a bad girl." I shrug and wink in a moment of brazen boldness.

"Oh!" He grabs me around my shoulders and squeezes. "I'm in for a good night, then!"

The laughter is spattered with wolf whistles and gentle innuendo. Funnily enough, it's quite reassuring. Boys being boys and all that. It's been a very long time since I've got cat calls and whistles. I don't know if it's something that naturally comes with being a mum, or if it happened in reaction to being so harshly dumped, but my clothing choice went from fancy to frumpy very quickly and any kind of attention from men, wanted or not, stopped years ago.

"Now, I didn't realise I'd picked up a bad girl," Thunder purrs. We walk down a long corridor. "Am I in danger?"

"Of course not," I reply with a twinkle in my eye. "I'll be gentle."

"Oh, please no—I like it rough."

And once again I'm tongue-tied. It seems I'm destined to always be the one on the back foot with him.

"Now, I promise there's no ulterior motive here," he says as we walk out into the street to be met by a large, serious-looking vehicle, a Range Rover or something like that. "But shall we go back to my hotel? We can drink at the bar, but can escape to my room if I start getting hounded."

"Sure, that's fine by me."

I'm a big girl—if he makes advances I can resist. If I want to resist, that is.

He opens the door of the vehicle for me, then closes it once I'm sat inside. How gentlemanly. Seconds later he hops in whilst cursing. "Step on it, mate, there's a stampeding hoard of fans heading this way."

He reaches for the seatbelt to strap himself in and I turn my head to look out of the back window. Sure enough, a group which seems to be largely made up of girls is legging it down the street towards us.

"I came out of a different entrance to avoid this." He shakes his head. "But there was a lookout who spotted me."

The driver engages the engine and pulls off at quite a lick, pushing me harder into the upholstery.

"Sorry." He lays his hand over mine. "All the fun of being famous."

I see the heaviness in his eyes. Folk often complain that celebrities don't know they're born and that they should accept the invasion of their privacy as a side effect of what they do. After all, they make a lot of money, right? I've never bought into that way of thinking. Everyone is entitled to some privacy. It must be very wearying to have to deal with journalists and crazed fans all the time.

"It's okay. Must get annoying, though."

"Oh, yeah. I mean, it comes with the job, but some of the things the fans will do to just get close to me is kinda disturbing."

"Yeah," the driver calls out. "Only the other week some girl threw herself under my wheels to get Thunder's autograph."

"Oh my God, was she all right?"

"Yeah, Don was only doing about five miles an hour at the time. She bounced off." Thunder sighs.

"Thunder got out, gave her an autograph, and she skipped off like nothing had happened." Don laughs. "I mean, it's funny, but what if I'd been going any quicker? Doesn't bear thinking about, really."

There's a moment's silence as we all consider what could have happened.

"What possesses someone like that? To throw all common sense out of the window?" I ask, shaking my head.

"It's some kind of mania, I think. Like, the guy following me around Asda asking me to sign his cabbage for him was not in his right mind. He got quite aggressive when it turned out I didn't have a pen. Then there was that OAP stalker. She got herself arrested in the end."

"Bloody hell, what a nightmare."

"Well, the majority are nice, mostly sane, and if I put on a hat and dress like a chav no one even knows it's me. Just I can't really do that at a concert, can I?"

"No, that's true. It'd probably get a few raised eyebrows anyway."

Amy would hate it in that fervent way teenagers do. Everything is so clean cut when you're thirteen. There are alternative people and there are chavs and also old people. By old she means twenty years and above. Everyone fits in those categories and there is no overlap. Oh, for the simplicity of youth.

"I once contemplated growing out my hair and losing the lightning bolt. Made the mistake of tweeting about it. Oh wow. Who knew so many people had such strong feelings about hair?"

"Oh, I hear you. My daughter feels ridiculously passionate about eyebrows of all things. I don't get it at all, but then I never really have."

"Too cool for school, huh, Josie?" Thunder winks.

"Oh, Lord, I wish." I laugh. "I've never been cool."

Just then the Range Rover stops and Thunder quickly takes off his seatbelt.

"Okay, let's get into the hotel before any more fans attack." He leaps out, and before I can open my door he's opening it and grabbing me.

He wraps an arm around me and walks us quickly towards a side entrance. There's a lot of talking and people around but I can't really tell who or what since Thunder is towering over me to my right and Don is blocking out the view to my left whilst talking rapidly into a phone. We reach the fire exit and it's opened for us immediately, then slammed shut behind us.

"Christ almighty, they get everywhere. Damn journos. You all right, Josie?"

"Yeah, I'm okay, I couldn't really see anything. I wasn't sure what was going on."

"Well there was a group of fans waiting, but in amongst them were some members of the less than esteemed press. That's why I route marched us through it all. I don't want to pay their damn wages for another week. You know they just make the shit up that goes with the photos they take?"

"Yeah." I nod.

"Yeah, so they get more money than me a week for taking a crap photo and making some scandal up to go with it. Fucking scum. Do you mind if we go straight up to my room? They'll be hounding me all night otherwise."

"Okay, then, that's fine." If this is all a scheme to get me into bed with him, it's working quite well. Although he really doesn't have to try this hard. All he has to do is ask!

"Oh, you're a star, Josie. Thank you so much." He leans in and kisses my cheek. Don accompanies us in the lift and only turns to leave once we're in Thunder's room. Maybe he'll stay out in the corridor all night? I don't know how all this works.

"Welcome to my humble abode." He bows with florid exaggeration.

It's not terribly humble. There's a huge living room area, with a giant bed up at the other end of the room. I guess the door to the left leads to a bathroom. "Wow, this is impressive."

"There are a few perks to this business. Have a seat, make yourself comfy. Do you want a drink?" He pulls off his beanie and jacket and throws them on the chair by the door.

"Oh, erm, yes please."

"There's some beers in the fridge. I think there might be some champagne in there, too. What do you fancy?"

"A beer will be fine. I don't really like champagne."

"Me either—it's all fizz and pop with no real taste." He grabs two cans and brings them over to the sofa. I realise suddenly how far away this is from my normal life. Swanky hotel, hot young man, and out after eight on a Friday night. This is definitely very much out of my comfort zone.

Thunder deposits the cans on the oak coffee table and drops down with little finesse into the seat beside me.

"So, hey." He looks me straight in the eye. Lord, he's gorgeous.

"Hey." I giggle, trying hard to stare right back, but duck my head as his gaze becomes too intense. "Fancy meeting you here."

"Fancy," he responds, reaching out and grabbing his can. "I'm so sorry for all the arsing around. I'd have much preferred to have taken you out for a good meal and wined you and dined you the proper way but, I'm afraid, this is as close as it gets."

He opens the can and takes a long swig.

"It's fine. I understand. I—well, I'm still not totally sure this is all real." I shake my head gently.

"Oh, it certainly is real. I can pinch you if you'd like." He puts his free hand on my arm and I squeak in advance of him exerting any pressure.

"But I actually think kissing you would work better."

His face is right in front of me and his lips are pressing on mine before I realise and I'm kissing back deeply. His lips are soft and giving, but his kiss is hard and demanding. The contrast makes my mind whirl and my heart beat faster.

I've not felt so turned on in more years than I care to admit. His hands rest on my hips, long fingers extended, begging me for more. I claw at his chest, not sure if I'm pulling him in or pushing him away. There's part of me that's trying desperately to escape. That corner of my brain that has the photos of his conquests stored up, the articles they were attached to ready to quote.

But I don't want to listen to that. This hot, sexy man is kissing me, arousing me in a way I've only ever experienced in my dreams before ... What would I gain from pushing him away? Sure, he's a player, but he's going to be out of my life tomorrow, so why not have fun while he's here?

I wrap my fingers in his T-shirt and pull him closer. That appears to be his cue to slide his hands up my back and deepen the kiss even further. Am I breathing? Am I kissing? I can't tell the difference anymore. I don't want to. I need more of his kiss more than I need the air.

"Convinced it's real yet?" He runs his hand over my shoulder, pulling my dress strap down with his soft touch.

"Erma ..." I gasp and pull in a deep breath. "It's getting more and more dream like."

"How often do you snog me in your dreams?" His lips turn up in a cheeky little smirk.

"Now that would be telling." I look down between our bodies as my cheeks heat.

Thunder lifts my chin with his finger until I'm looking him straight in the eyes. "Well then, are the real kisses or the dream kisses better?"

I lick my lips nervously. "Real, I think."

"Only think?" He shakes his head gently, grinning all the while.

"Well, I've got limited experience to go on so far," I reply, finding bravery from his lusty gaze.

"But that was my best kissing." He pouts.

I laugh and quickly kiss his pout. "But you only kissed my lips. You kiss other places in my dreams."

Thunder raises an eyebrow with surprise, then he laughs. "Oh well then, let's give you something else to work on." Dipping forward he kisses where my jawline meets my ear then trails gentle kisses lower until he's nestling into my neck and adding nibbles to the mix.

I let out a soft moan when his nibbles centre on my pulse point. They deepen and get harder until it's a bite and a suck and I am melted goo in his arms.

"That's cheating, it's supposed to just be kissing," I gasp, trying to regain the upper hand.

He drops lower, kisses softly, then digs his teeth into the flesh over my clavicle. "This is heavy metal kissing."

And I won't want to be kissed any other way from here on in.

Holding my arms down beside my body he kisses across my chest in a meandering line. I'm trapped, deliciously so, and my heart pounds harder as his lips caress the skin over it. Grabbing and pulling down the top of my dress with one hand, he skims his kisses lower. My heart stops. What's he going to do next?

He leans back, still holding onto the top of my dress, and looks at me questioningly. I nod. I want him to carry on. Thunder pulls the neckline of my dress even lower until he can pop out my bra-clad bust and tuck my dress under it.

I drag in a deep breath. My chest expands and pushes my breasts more proudly forward. I release it slowly, controlling the panic bubbling and swirling inside of me. No one has seen me less than fully dressed in so many years. What's he going to think of my body?

Thunder is completely focused on the revealed flesh. I don't know if he has even realised how nervous I am. He doesn't stop at the dress—he dips his hand in between my boob and the black lace of my bra.

My nervous gulp morphs into a desire-filled moan as his fingers mould and clasp my breast, his palm brushing my hard nipple. He pulls up and extracts the flesh from its cage. He strokes it reverently with his thumb then extends his neck to plant his lips on me again. Thunder wiggles on the sofa to trail those kisses lower down and curses when his knees knock mine.

"Going down." He chuckles and kneels on the floor. Pushing my knees apart, he crawls between them, meets my gaze and winks. Before I can think or speak he grabs my naked breast once more and his lips gently caress and press down over the swell of my boob, only stopping when they find my nipple. Thunder opens his mouth and takes the whole of it inside, sucking and slurping and groaning in equal measure.

I can't stop the keening noises I make. His strong sucking action pulls through my body and I feel the desire building and pooling between my thighs. It's so strong, so overwhelming that I reach out and grab his shoulders, desperately needing something to hold on to.

Thunder's eager sucks are interwoven with nibbles. The graze and nip of his teeth stings, but that somehow heightens the pleasure. Without taking his mouth away from me, he eases his hand into the other cup of my bra and releases my second breast to sit against his hand, the underwire of my bra cradling and digging into the underside of both boobs.

Redirecting his attention, he kisses over the hillock of the newly freed breast, seeking out the nipple to suck and nibble and bite. I run my fingers through his hair and across the shaved side of his head, tracing the outline of the lightning bolt, finally accepting that this is happening.

Thunder traces a hand over my waist, skims his fingers down my thighs and stops when he encounters naked flesh. I may be above him, might be positionally the one in control, but inside I'm anything but. I'm completely submissive to his whims and desires. I've given myself over to lust.

What a relief.

It's hard work being grown up and in control all the damn time. Everyone needs the opportunity to just let go.

He rucks up my skirt and I push myself towards him, craving more of his touch. He fans his fingers out across my thigh and I mentally urge them higher and higher. Maybe he hears my internal cries as he slips his fingers up and the tips soon encounter the gusset of my knickers. They move gently, caressing my mound and catching my labia through the cotton. I'm sure Thunder can feel how wet my knickers are, and I am even hotter and wetter underneath them.

I'm disappointed when his lips leave my breasts, but when they reappear on my inner thigh just above my knee I'm excited by the change of location.

His lips follow the inside of my thigh, and as he pushes higher his shoulders push against my knees and press them wider. My breath escapes in rushed pants of anticipation.

Thunder drags the material of the knickers to one side, exposing my wet, engorged pussy. I flush, a little apprehensive at him seeing me so intimately.

His first licks are tentative, I think, because of my position on the sofa. I scooch forward, my butt against the leather making a high pitched squeaking sound.

He chuckles and thanks me, taking any embarrassment out of the situation. His kisses continue in a far less hesitant manner. Splitting my lips with his tongue, he delves deeper. It's so sexy, I am awash with passion and rock against his face, wanting to feel the push and pull of his tongue inside me.

Moments later I change my mind as he finds the little nub of my clit. I want him to keep doing that, hitting that spot, strumming and building the tempo just with that rhythm. I convey that to him by reaching down and winding my fingers in his hair, holding him close.

He takes the direction, continuing to run his tongue up and down, making me whimper and whine with the building aches, and the desperation for release heightens. I forget everything but my need and thrust myself up against his mouth, faster and faster until I come with a loud groan.

I let go, my whole body relaxing in response to the release. Thunder scrambles up, perches a knee on the sofa between my thighs and leans in to kiss me. I smell my musk, then taste it, a bolt of lust running through me again at the reminder of what he's just done.

"I wanna fuck you so bad," he pants between kisses.

"Then fuck me," I reply, "fuck me now."

It takes him seconds to open his jeans and push them down. I guess he had a condom in his pocket because the next thing I hear is the crinkle of a packet and when I look he's pulling a condom free.

Looking down I see how eager he is, his cock hard and straining forward, the tip gleaming with pre-cum. I split my legs wider for him, desperate to feel him inside me.

He doesn't take it slowly at all, but then he knows how wet I am. He drives into me forcefully and I yelp my enjoyment as he stretches and fills me.

"Jesus, Josie," he groans. "You're so wet."

"You did it to me," I reply, wrapping my arms around his waist and pulling him closer.

"Oh, I've only just started," Thunder growls and thrusts hard into me several times in rapid succession, taking my breath away with the power, pleasure rolling through me. I drag my nails down his back and he fucks harder.

"Fuck, fuck," he chants, pushing his nose under my hair and burying his face in my neck. He peppers it with kisses and nibbles my earlobe. His pants tickle and I'm surrounded by his desire, consumed by his need.

Every part of me wants him to come. I want to feel his joy, his every move is warm ecstasy and I'm perfectly content to let him use me in any way he needs. I hold onto him through his varied thrusts—I know he's trying to make the experience last and I am very happy about that.

When he builds up the speed further, lifts his head back and curves himself away from me, I know he's close. My hands rest on his hips and my eyes that had been closed languidly through the rapture, flutter open. His face is taut with need and my body tightens when I realise how far lost in lust he is.

I watch him come. He tightens and holds himself within me, grunts, then groans. His jaw slackens and flows into a soft smile as his orgasm melts away. Thunder relaxes and rests his body on me, his chest heaving with exertion.

Our combined breathing is all I can hear and I revel in the post-sex glow. I'd forgotten how good it feels. The euphoria of mutual pleasure.

"Fancy a pizza?" he asks.

"Hell yeah!" I reply.

The contentment is complete.

CHAPTER THREE

"Oh, it is good to be able to enjoy my favourite pizza topping without fear of ridicule for a change," Thunder sighs.

"I know what you mean." I wave my slice of ham and pineapple topped deep pan in the air. "Amy won't even tolerate the idea of fruit on a pizza. So we always have to get flippin' pepperoni."

"The band nag me so much about how wrong it is I've given up ordering it for myself because of the bloody aggro. Bastards." Thunder tilts his head back and dangles his slice just above his mouth then shoots forward to grab the dangling tip between his teeth. His moan is sensual as he chews.

"The things we do for love, huh?" I mutter before taking a huge bite of the delicious pizza.

He nods and continues chewing.

On the grand scale of 'things I expect to be doing on a Friday night', lying naked in a posh hotel king-size bed, eating pizza with Thunder Jackson is not something high up on the list. The fact that I'm feeling pretty relaxed and not at all anxious about it is even crazier.

Thunder is genuinely a nice guy, and I'm thoroughly enjoying my time with him. Even the seemingly mundane conversation. The sex is amazing, too. That's another thing I never expected on a Friday night.

"How old did you say your kid was again?" he asks, after a long swig of beer.

"She's thirteen—turns fourteen next month and has been acting like a middle-aged woman since she was about three." I smile.

"God, you must have been an infant yourself when you had her," he exclaims.

"Flatterer." I shake my head gently. "I was twenty-one, actually."

"I started Black Tranquillity when I was twenty-one. It feels like we've been together forever, not just a few years. God, I can't imagine the responsibility of having a child. It's bad enough looking after my boys in the band."

"Oh, you just have to get on with it." I gulp down a mouthful of ice cold beer.

"How long have you been on your own with her?"

"Amy's dad walked out on me before she was born. Turns out he was just in it for a fun time. When I announced my pregnancy, he left me."

"Shitbag," Thunder cursed. "How could anyone do that? Jesus."

Clearly Thunder doesn't read what is written about him in the ladies' mags, since I've seen at least two articles claiming him to be the runaway father of babies. Either that or he's just deeply in denial.

"I've let it go, Thunder. The guy wouldn't have been good for me or Amy anyway. He showed his true colours. It's hard on her to know her dad left before she was born, but it could have been much worse."

Thunder nodded. "My father was an evil fucking rat bastard. Beat the shit out of my mum for years. It was only when he hit me—I was only like, six, I think—that she left him."

"I'm sorry to hear that." I reach out and squeeze the top of his arm.

"Well, like you say, it could have been a lot worse. Me and Mum were just fine on our own. We looked after each other. It wasn't easy for her, though. You're well brave to have brought your kid up on your own."

"I have the help of my family and friends. I'm not totally in it alone, thank God. Now I know why they say it takes a community to bring up a child. I bet your mum is proud of bringing up a world famous metal star."

"She was." He drops his last slice of pizza back into the box. "Sadly she died a few months after we hit it big. She was in a car accident."

"Oh, God, I didn't realise. I shouldn't have said anything."

"No, no, it's fine—you weren't to know. I mean, it still hurts, of course. I don't think you ever get over something like that, you know? I'll always be grieving. But it gets easier to bear with time and I don't mind talking about her at all."

"I know what you mean. I lost my mother when Amy was little and God, I still miss her so very much." I drag in a deep breath as the grief rolls over me like a wave and tears prick at the corners of my eyes.

Thunder scrambles over the duvet, kicking the pizza box and the scraps onto the floor and envelops me in a huge hug.

We cling together in silence, feeling and appreciating each other's grief. The physical presence of someone who knows the pain is all I need. No words can make it better so we just hug, offering solace through the storm.

"Thunder," I whisper, "I'm going to have to do something really mumsy now."

He looks puzzled when I pull away, fling myself across the bed and dangle over the edge.

"The pizza box on the floor was worrying me."

Thunder laughs explosively and I smile even though he can't see. It's such a joyful sound, I can't help it.

"It's okay, though," I continue. "There's no smeared cheese and tomato on the carpet." I reach down and pick up the discarded crusts and odds and scrape them into the box.

"You have a beautiful arse," he remarks and I squeak when he slaps it.

"Thanks." The word escapes in a short high pitched gasp. "If you like it, why are you being mean to it?"

"Did you not like that?" Suddenly there's a tension in the air.

"Well, no, I kinda did like it," I reply. "I was just wondering, that's all."

"Oh, good. I blame it on whatever drummer genes I have left." He gently slaps one cheek then the other in a rhythmic fashion. "I always wanted to be a drummer, but sadly I'm a bit shit at it."

"It feels like you're pretty good at it."

The smacks vary in hardness and I can definitely tell he's working a beat.

"Why, thank you. I am very good at playing the butt, just not so great on drums, and no one would let me play the butt on stage. Too many safety concerns, apparently."

I laugh and it mixes and melds with his, but there's a kinda sexy image in my head of being placed over his knee, legs split around his waist and my bottom being played like the bongos in front of a huge crowd. My cheeks heat at the thought.

"The other thing is, I get very easily distracted." One hand continues to tap out a beat whilst the fingers of his other slip down between my cheeks and into my wetness. I moan when his fingers cup around and catch my clit. He repeats the action, moving that hand up and down, coaxing more moans from my lips. "It's very, very sexy, but apparently this doesn't count as music you can play on stage."

"Shame," I gasp, "you're very good."

"Cheers Josie." He squeezes my buttock. "I'd like to continue too but my dick is hard and it's distracting me. Mind if I fuck you now?"

"Please, go ahead," I acquiesce.

He scrambles about on the bed. I hear the crinkling of foil again, then yelp when suddenly he pulls on my hips, settling his thighs between mine I put my hands down on the floor for balance when he pushes me further forward to expose my wetness to his sight.

"Oh, man," he whispers. "So fucking beautiful."

I honestly can't imagine what he's going to do next. Surely our bodies can't fit together with me dangling off the bed like this? So I'm especially surprised but joyful when I feel his cock pressing up between my labia until the tip is lodged inside me. He wiggles and jiggles, and my knees come to rest on the bed, like I'm in position to do it doggy style, but this way I feel more like a wheelbarrow and he's more behind me now, I can't feel as much of him against my thighs.

It's quite precarious, but Thunder's hands on my hips keep me in place as he slides even deeper.

"Fuck," he groans. "Is this okay for you?"

"Yes," I gasp. "I'm balanced on my hands. God, you're so deep."

"I feel like I'm totally buried inside you," he replies, "it's awesome."

He pulls back slowly and pushes forward again at the same pace. It's almost indescribable, it's so good. I can feel the whole length of him inside me, the pressure sparking off ripples of joy that roll through my body.

With each pump he moves a little faster until he finds a rhythm to suit him. It's not as fast and frenzied as the last fuck and I relish in feeling every movement he makes. My arms ache but I'm trying hard to ignore that and concentrate on where our bodies join.

"This is awesome, but I think it's time for a different position." I guess Thunder noticed how I was moving my weight from one hand to another. He moves back and I whimper at the loss of his fullness inside me. "Get up here."

I scramble backwards and onto the bed, still on hands and knees. He grabs my hips and pulls me way back, and I squeal in surprise. I gather the duvet in my hands and try to keep some kind of balance. Part of me is impressed with his strength—to drag me across the bed like this takes a fair bit of muscle—but most of me is just wondering what the fuck is going to happen next.

I come to rest with my butt up against Thunder's pelvis. The soft hair of his pubis tickle against m and revel in the warmth of his skin. He takes one hand off my hip and his knuckles graze against my wet, open pussy as he guides his cock up and inside me.

"That's it," he groans. "Fuck, your arse is beautiful."

"I think you said that already," I reply without thinking, earning myself a slap across the buttock.

"Well you did!" I squeak and he slaps me again. The warmth radiates through me, turning sharp pain to mellow rapture. I purr in satisfaction.

"God, woman, you like that." He thrusts forward, digging his fingers into my hips.

"Seems I do." I wonder if he can hear the surprise in my voice.

"Jesus, Josie. You're so bloody awesome." He fucks harder and I feel the vibration through my whole body. There is something so rough and primal about sex in this position. I growl and press against him, driving him all the deeper, making the slight sting of my slapped buttock spark painfully, which in turn makes all my internal muscles clench. Thunder whimpers and curses and moves one hand to catch hold of my hair. Wrapping it around his fist, he pulls my head back and regains control again.

It's my turn to whimper. My scalp is on fire and for the shortest moment I want it to stop, but then the combination of the ache of my pulled hair and the fullness of Thunder inside me sends ecstasy coursing everywhere and suddenly I don't want it to ever stop.

"Fuck!" I exclaim. "Fuck yes, Thunder, fuck!"

It makes no sense but I can't stop speaking, the words just fall out in a jumbled mess at each thrust. It's like I'm so full, so close to bursting, that I need to find a release somehow and that is through the babble of words, squeaks and screams that escape on every slap of his body against mine.

I become aware of his voice, mumbling low. I can't understand the words at first but the same rhythmic mantra continues and grows louder and louder until it's fully audible over my own ecstatic noises.

"Gonna come, gonna come, gonna come." He screams the words and the last notes hang in the air and entangle with my own joyous "Yes!" at his ejaculation.

I collapse onto my stomach and Thunder slumps against my arse. Finally he pulls back and slumps onto the bed beside me. Turning onto my side, I snuggle up into him and we cling together. My head over his heart, I can hear it thundering away. A smile creeps across my face as I digest my own secret meaning of his name—the roaring of his heartbeat, excited by me.

I'm still horny, so I press myself harder against Thunder and lift my knee up to rest on his hip, lewdly splitting my legs and offering an open invite. I'm glad he takes the hint and slips his fingers down to my spread thighs and pushes a couple inside me, pumping in and out until I moan and my knee shakes.

His thumb sits comfortably on my clit and circles while he fingers me. I tighten and clench as pleasure whizzes through my blood 'til I feel lightheaded with it. My breathing is laboured, my cheeks are hot and my whole body vibrates with need. Thunder continues his methodical, deliberate movements. I can hear how wet I am, can even smell my light, feminine musk.

"Gonna come!" It's my turn to gasp out the words of warning and Thunder continues to do exactly what he's doing, thank God. The slightest change of pace could halt this ecstasy in its tracks but nothing is going to stop me now.

I dig my nails into his back, the delight bursting out of me. I roar against his chest, bucking and shaking as the orgasm shoots through me.

"Good girl," Thunder whispers, cradling me closer with the arm that lies beneath me. "Good girl." He continues to stroke my clit, extending the rapture for a second longer each time until it becomes far too sensitive and I shake him off.

He slowly removes his fingers, I bring my thigh down off his hip to ease my muscles and he raises those fingers to his mouth and sucks my cum off them with a leisurely wink. I gulp. It's so sexy. All of a sudden, there's a spark of yet more desire in the pit of my stomach. I can't believe it. Surely I've had enough?

"You are going to stay here with me tonight, aren't you?" Thunder asks, dropping his hand down to rest on my hip.

"I wasn't planning to," I reply honestly, "but then I wasn't planning to shag you either and I've done that. Twice."

"You weren't planning to?" His voice has a quizzical twang to it.

"Nope, I wasn't even really expecting to meet you again if I'm totally honest."

"Does this mean I seduced you?" I can feel his smile as his cheek pulls against the side of my head.

"It does indeed," I reply, kissing his chest.

"Oh, I must still have it, then." He chuckles. "So, you're staying, right?"

"Mmm-hmm." I nod gently. "Currently I couldn't move even if I wanted to."

I trace a finger over the licks of flames that are tattooed across his chest, over his heart and around his nipples. They seem to ripple up close, like real flames. I wouldn't say I was a fan of tattoos but they sit well on Thunder's skin. Beautiful decoration.

"Know whatcha mean." He yawns. "It's been a long day."

"I don't know how you've got the energy to do anything after bouncing around on stage like that."

"Oh, it's all about motivation." He kisses the top of my head. "I've been very motivated tonight."

"The power of pineapple on pizza."

"Something like that," he agrees, squeezing me close. "Something like that."

CHAPTER FOUR

I wake with a start. There's someone in my bed with his arm strewn casually across my middle. There are two giveaways that it's a he—the hair on his arm, tickling against my hand resting on top of it, and the erect cock pressing up to my arse.

I draw in a deep breath to calm down. It's Thunder. I'm in his bed in his hotel room. I'm so used to waking up on my own that his presence truly unnerved me at first. My heart is still thumping hard but I'm not scared anymore. Now it's because I'm so aware of his hard body all around me contrasting with my softness.

Torn between moving and staying completely still, I give a little wiggle as the stiffness in my back from being in the same position for so long becomes too much. Thunder groans and pushes harder into me. He curls his arm around my waist and squeezes, moulding me against him.

Is he awake? I can't tell so I freeze. As desperate as I am to feel more of him, I don't want to wake him up. What if he's a grumpy riser? Now I wish I'd paid more attention when Amy read out random and apparently interesting facts from her magazines. I might know his morning routine if I'd paid attention. It's crazy what details teenage fans seem to find fascinating about random celebs.

He stirs further, but this time his hand strays with purpose. He moves it higher and grabs my breast, his thumb lazily sweeping over my nipple.

"Mmm." I relax back into him, confident now that he's awake.

"Morning, sunshine," he purrs, kissing the nape of my neck and plucking at my nipple. It hardens to his touch.

"Morning," I reply huskily. "Sleep well?"

"Yeah." He slides his hand down over my stomach and lower, into my pubic hair. "You?"

"Really good, thanks."

His fingers slip down and I part my thighs so he can cup my pubis and rest his fingers between my damp lips.

"But the waking up is better," I gasp as he rubs my clit. I can't believe how turned on I already am.

"I'm usually grumpy when I get up, but I'm horny because I'm getting up today." He presses his cock into my bum even harder. "If you get what I mean."

"I feel you, bro." I chuckle.

"Ooh, kinky." He laughs and I roll to face him.

"You know what I mean." I prod him in the chest.

"I know, I know, just teasing." He dips his head to capture my lips with his. For a split second I worry about morning breath, but he's kissing me so deeply it really mustn't be a problem, and soon all I can think of is how much I want him to fuck me.

"It worked too, you're facing me now so I can do this." He shoves me in the centre of my chest and I fall to my back with a squeal. Before I can yell at him for scaring me like that, he's between my thighs, grabbing my hands and holding them down beside my head.

"Bastard," I exclaim with a giggle.

"Cheeky minx." He leans forward and blows a raspberry at the centre of my chest, making me squeal. He continues; kissing, blowing raspberries across to my armpit and back, until I am begging him to stop through the laughter. I'm very, very ticklish.

All the time he holds my hands down, I'm trapped and laughing my head off.

"Surrender?" he asks.

"Yes." I gasp as he nips and nibbles at the upper curve of my boob. "Yes, yes, yes!"

"Gonna be a good girl now?" He bites down, just above my nipple, his teeth digging into my flesh.

"God, yes." I groan and press my groin up towards him. The pain is overwhelmingly pleasurable. I'm not even sure how that works.

Thunder stops biting and kisses instead. "That's better. Now keep your hands where I've put them."

He sits back on his heels and looks down at me. I'm sure I look a mess—bed head, red cheeks, sleep-sticky eyes, and probably those wrinkle lines you get from lying on sheets in the same position for a while, but all I can see in his gaze is lust.

He reaches between his own thighs and strokes his cock whilst looking at me. I am an object, something to be desired and wanted. It makes my heart leap and my body tighten with arousal to be that to him. To be his. Even if it's just for this brief moment of time.

I push down the wave of sadness which comes with the realisation that this one night is all we can realistically have together. I can't think about that yet.

"Fucking hell, you're gorgeous. A work of art. Stay there, don't move."

He scrambles off the bed, picks up his jeans and fishes his phone and a condom out of the pocket.

"Okay." He jumps back on his knees between my thighs. "Please can I take a photo of you?"

"Erm, well—" I really want to protest that my hair is a mess and I must look terrible, but instead I shrug. Clearly he doesn't think that way. "Okay then, sure."

"Thanks." He presses at his phone screen a few times then aims it at me. I smile. I watch the concentration on his face as he moves the camera to capture the perfect angle. His hair flops forward over one of his eyes and I really want to push it out of his face, grab his cheeks and kiss him and kiss him and kiss him some more. But I don't. I lie still, arms flat against the bedsheet because he told me to leave them there.

"Got it." He flashes the screen my way. I nod—it looks pretty good from a distance. He throws the phone down onto the bed beside us. "Now, play with your clit while I get this condom sorted."

I have never masturbated in front of another person before, so I very hesitantly reach down my body and rest my hand over my pussy, my eyes clamped closed. I don't want to see him watching me. There is a freedom in his command somehow. I'm not doing it, in a way. He is. This gives me the bravery to press a finger in between my folds and seek out the moistness pooled there. I push my pointer finger inside me and gather up more of my nectar to rub over my clit, so my finger pad glides over it more easily.

I relax the more I touch myself—the bliss coursing through me makes me want to wank more, building up the need to come.

"Open your eyes, Josie."

I flutter open my lashes and meet his heated gaze. Thunder's pupils are large and the green of his eyes is darker than I've seen it before. I continue to brazenly finger myself as I stare deep into him, past the beautiful exterior into his human, vulnerable core. Gulping, I flutter my lashes a little bit against the welling tears. Deep inside I know this is the start of our goodbye.

"Keep touching yourself, Josie, please," he begs, pressing closer, brushing his hair-covered legs against the soft dampness of my inner thighs until his hardness is pressing against my fingertips. He slips inside me without any resistance, and I wrap my legs around him, pulling him close. His pubis pushes down on the back of my hand, trapping it against my clit.

Not a word is spoken, our bodies say it all. I grab onto his waist with my spare hand and he dips his head until our lips meet, softly at first then the kiss deepens and becomes rougher and more urgent as his thrusts quicken in pace.

It's a terrible conundrum. I'm caught between never wanting this to stop and really needing to come. It doesn't matter how long you try to hold on, pleasure eventually reaches its crescendo. Thunder's lips pull away from mine as his body tightens and throbs. He's close.

"Come with me," he gasps. "Please, Josie."

"I'm close," I groan, "hold on for me."

"Always."

I squeeze my eyes tighter, concentrating on the small, powerful nub beneath my fingertip. One tiny area of my body gives so much enjoyment, it's amazing really. Thunder's cock jumps within me and I whimper. I'm so close. I can feel his weight on me, the tension in his body, echoing my own. I rub with quick, determined strokes, arousal suddenly swelling and peaking like a flood.

"Now!" I cry and from the small, measured pushes he begins to thrust hard and fast and I come equally hard and fast, screaming his name. His grunts and exclamations join and blend with my own. I gasp and gulp, tears flowing. Ecstasy burst the banks and I just let go.

Thunder kisses the tears from my cheeks. He rolls to his side and pulls me tightly into him. No words, just unconditional comfort. As my heartbeat returns to normal and my tears dry, I take in a shuddering breath. Being a mature, responsible adult I really need to get a grip. Why on earth is such a casual encounter affecting me like this?

"Josie, I'm sorry, baby, but I'm going to have to call Don to give you a lift home. The guys are on the tour bus already waiting for me."

"Oh, okay, that's fine–wait, how do you know they're on the bus?"

"I had several not so pleasant messages on my phone, but I wasn't going to let them stop this." He beams.

There's suddenly a loud, insistent hammering at the door and everything happens in a whirlwind. I grab my clothes and dress in the bathroom, combing my hair with my fingers and spritzing perfume on me and last night's outfit. I check my phone—just one message from Claire to tell me that Amy is fine and they're going to the cinema. I'm glad—it'll give me a few hours to get in, get changed and gather myself before she starts asking questions.

When I re-emerge, Thunder is fully dressed and arguing with a familiar-looking dude. I think it's Grant, the drummer.

"Just let me say bye, okay, dude? Look, she's here now."

"Get on with it, we'll be fucking late at this rate. I hate not having time for a full rehearsal."

"Hey." Thunder runs over and wraps me in a hug. "I gotta go. It's been wild."

"It sure has," I reply with a big grin. We kiss deeply.

"I'll message you, promise. Bye, Josie. Don will be up in a minute. Wait here for him."

"Bye, Thunder."

His bandmate literally drags him away from me and out of the door. I feel empty and deeply sad.

"It was just sex." I say out loud. It doesn't really make me feel any better. Luckily there's a knock on the door. My lift home has arrived.

CHAPTER FIVE

"So, what's he like? How did it go? Did you kiss?" Amy bounces up and down as she barrages me with questions.

"He's nice, funny, clever. It went well. I had a good time, and ham and pineapple on my pizza, and the rest is none of your business, nosey."

"You kissed! You kissed! I know you did. Oh, I'm so happy for you, Mum. You need a man in your life."

"Pfft." I drop the potato I was cutting into the pan of water on the cooker. "I don't need a man at all, Amy."

"Yeah right, Mum, whatever. When you going to see him again?"

"Dunno." I shrug. "We've not arranged another meeting. Might not even happen."

"Aw, don't say that. I bet he'll ring you soon for a second date. Anyway, I'm off to my room. I need to Skype with Kirsty."

"What? You only just left her five minutes ago."

"I know, but we've got important stuff to discuss in private."

"Bryan Harper," I yell after her up the stairs.

"Oh, shut up!" she yells back. She hates the fact I know the name of her crush. Oh, to be thirteen again. Not a care in the world. Saying that, I feel uncomfortably like a teenager as I have checked my phone approximately a billion times an hour in case I missed the notification of him texting me. I've not. Not had even a word from him.

Yet.

He's probably forgotten all about me.

The rest of the day passes slowly, with me in a turtleneck. When I looked in the bathroom mirror at home I saw the bruises left by Thunder's heavy metal kisses. I spent a good while admiring them, but there was no way I was letting Amy see them.

I keep prodding them through my top, the spark of pain a vivid reminder that it all really did happen. So finally when I roll into bed at a ridiculously early hour, I decide to take the initiative. I'm a strong, independent woman. I can text him first if I want to.

Had fun last night. Missing the pizza and laughter. Hope your gig went well. Josie x

I toss and turn, checking and re-checking the phone screen, closing the cover and checking again. It's gone midnight when I finally get a response.

Missing you too x

It's not exactly the world's longest missive, but it's something. He misses me! Maybe there's some kind of hope we'll get together in the end. My mum always said I was a hopeless romantic.

***

"How could you!" Amy bursts into the living room, shaking her phone vigorously.

I don't react at first—I'm quite used to these outbursts of teenage angst. Usually they're nothing to do with me and are generally in relation to some nugget of gossip from her school mates or a controversial YouTuber opinion.

"What's got you shook now?" I ask. Pretending I get the teenage lingo tends to lighten the atmosphere. She thinks I'm much too old to be cool.

"Oh, don't even try." She shakes the phone more violently in my direction. "Why didn't you tell me your date was with Thunder Jackson?"

"What? Wait, what?" I shake my head in confusion. How does Amy know that?

"Look!" She shoves her phone under my nose. "Don't deny it. The photos are right there."

And sure enough, there on the screen is a picture of Thunder with his arm around me. Damn, a journalist must have snapped us on our way into the hotel.

"Well, I didn't think it mattered who it was with," I reply, scrolling down the article.

"But it's Thunder, Mum. Jeez, you didn't even get me an autograph!"

"Well, I'll ask him to send you one if you like—holy crap!"

Suddenly there on the screen is a photo of me and Thunder kissing, but worse still, next to it is the photo he took of me. Heavily censored but still clearly me.

"Yeah, seems you did way more than kiss." Amy looks over my shoulder.

My jaw drops and I try to say something, but words just don't form.

"Oh, it's fine. I'm thirteen, Mum. I know people have sex."

"But, but, I mean, that photo was private!" I squeak.

"Yeah, that's bad form even for Thunder." She shrugs. "Sorry, Mum."

"Oh God, everyone will see this! Christ, what if Mr Donaldson sees it?" Full blown panic has set in.

"Don't worry!" Amy has gone from accusation mode to conciliation in a matter of moments. She can see I'm melting down. "It's just a photo and it's not like you put it out there on purpose or anything. I mean you can't even see anything bad."

"My tummy, my wobbly chin and bed head! That's bad enough. It's a naked image. Oh God, what if I lose my job?"

"You won't, Mum." Amy pats my arm. "It'll be fine. It'll blow over soon. I mean, last year that poor sixth former, Sophie Renson, well her nudes were splashed all over Facebook. She thought she was ruined, but no one even remembers it now. It's nothing, really."

"Yeah, no, yeah, you're probably right." I sigh. No use worrying Amy too. "It's only a picture."

Only a picture. A photo I let him take. One only he could have taken to the press. It's like I've been stabbed through the heart.

Amy takes her phone from me and smiles. "I'll go make you a brew, then we can watch a movie or something if you want."

"Can we watch *Dirty Dancing*?" I ask.

"Yeah, sure. I'll put a bag of popcorn in the microwave then, shall I?"

"Okay, cool."

Lord, it is bad. She's making me a cup of tea *and* allowing me to watch my favourite film without argument. I pick my phone up off the coffee table, ignore the pile of notifications, and click on to Thunder's message.

You absolute bastard. How could you? I trusted you. I can't believe you'd use me as a publicity stunt. Just fuck right off, pal. I don't want anything more to do with you.

I click send, then turn it off. I don't want to talk to anyone, text anyone—I don't want to even think of the outside world and the existence of that photo in the public domain.

***

"No one puts baby in the corner." I sniffle. This bit always makes me cry, but today there's more behind my tears than just the sappy movie.

"Erm, Mum, I think you might want to see this." Amy thrusts her phone at me.

"No, I don't." I shake my head. "I don't want to look at a phone or my laptop, I just want to pretend the outside world doesn't exist, thank you very much."

"But Mum. You need to see this." She shoves the phone into my hand and I sigh deeply before looking down.

"What?" I shake my head. "What am I looking at?"

"It's Thunder's Twitter feed, Mum. He's saying someone nicked his phone or data or something. He's condemning the site that posted those photos. Said he's pursuing it as a police matter."

"So he didn't send the photo to the press?"

"He says not. I know he's got a bad boy reputation, but it's well out of order to pass on nudes. And if he's going to the police it must be real, right?"

Sighing again, I pass her phone back to her. "I really don't know, Amy. People lie."

"They do, but I don't think he wanted to hurt you, Mum. He says in the last tweet. Apologises deeply to anyone hurt by the leaking of his phone images."

"Anyone? Does that mean there's loads of girls' nudes off his phone on the internet now then?"

"Not that I've seen." She shrugs. "I truly think this was an accident."

"That's why you're so brilliant, honey. You believe the best of everyone, bless your heart. Thanks for trying to cheer me up."

"Anytime, Mum. Love you."

"Love you too, champ."

She squeezes my arm and stands up. "I need to go do my chemistry homework, it'll take me ages. You be okay?"

"Yeah, no worries. Get your work done, hon."

When I'm sure she's upstairs, I let the tears fall. Just one time I let my hair down, just one time I go with my gut and don't deny myself like a responsible adult should, and I end up in the shit.

My reputation in ruins, my job on the line and my heart broken.

Yes, people's memories are short, but images stay on the internet forever. What am I going to do? Forever, now, when anyone looks me up online, that image is going to come up. It's always going to haunt me. Worse still, it will haunt Amy too.

I don't really want to look at it, but I grab my laptop and look up the article. Forearmed is forewarned. I need to know what's out there so I can defend myself when people bring it up. Which they will. Especially the girls at work. I just have to hope to God it doesn't get back to the boss.

To be fair, the photo is pretty flattering. The soft lighting, the angle he took it at—it's not terrible The censoring covers up a good chunk of my belly and boobs and my hair is spread out around me, not clumped all on one side. So at least I don't look too bad in it. The thing that really hurts me is the depth of emotion in my eyes.

I could have loved that man. I'm sure of it.

The article is badly jumbled together click bait. It mentions me only as Josie—I should thank the Lord for small mercies—and is basically a bundle of lies. It talks about a drink and drug-fuelled orgy, and the writer is seemingly shocked by my inclusion, even guessing my age wrong and aging me by ten years. And as if that isn't offensive enough, the article declares me not to be MILF material.

It makes my blood boil. I don't want to believe Thunder would dump me in it for something so juvenile, something so filled with lies. I shake my head as the tears drip on my cheeks.

"Pull yourself together!" I snap at myself. I've never been one for wallowing in self-pity. I am proactive.

I send a strongly worded email to the site, demanding they take down the article and photo or I'll sue them seven ways to hell and back. I'm not afraid to get my hands dirty.

Then I start to tackle the mess of messages and texts from friends and family offering sympathy, exclaiming shock, or in some cases both. It's amazing. I can go for weeks without interaction with anyone other than my daughter and my workmates. But suddenly everyone is wanting a piece of me.

I work hard to keep my responses neutral. I don't want any further information getting out there. I would have said I was being paranoid but that was before my naked body was splashed all over the 'net. I turn the sound off on my phone. I don't want to hear the notifications, and I certainly don't want to talk to anyone.

I get stuck into my housework, leaving my phone on the coffee table in the living room. Normally I keep it always in sight. Today I don't want the reminder.

I'm exhausted by the end of the day and my little two up, two down is sparkling clean.

When I head to bed, I'm a little disappointed to find that Thunder hasn't sent me a text in reply to mine. Stupid I know, but I thought at least he'd try to fix things. Maybe he is the bastard I accused him of being.

Amy has that gift of seeing the good in everyone. I was always like that too and I still try to be where I can, but I'm so much more jaded now. Especially when it comes to men. I've always wanted to believe that there were good men out there and that one day I'd meet mine.

I know I've only spent a little time with Thunder, but part of me was hoping he was my good man. It hurts to realise that I was so very, very wrong. All he wanted me for was the sex. Maybe someone to eat pizza with too. How could I have been so naïve?

You'd think I'd have learnt my lesson after Carl. He left me high and dry. I thought he was the one, but he was only using me. He wasn't completely useless—he gave me Amy after all, and Amy is my life.

I shouldn't have let Thunder get under my skin, but when I close my eyes all I can see is him, all I can feel is the ghost of his touch and all I can do is cry myself to sleep. I miss him. My heart hurts and it's all just too confusing for words.

***

Coffee is the only thing keeping me going. I dropped Amy at the bus stop so she could get the bus to school as usual, then headed into the office, where, just like I expected, I was talked about in hushed whispers. The day passed and I wasn't called into Mr Johnson's office even though I was on high alert just in case. I was thinking maybe Amy was right, but then just fifteen minutes before the end of my shift I'm summoned and it's as bad as I had imagined.

"But Sir, I didn't consent for this photo to be used online."

"It doesn't matter, you're our employee, Miss Black, and we can't have that association. We're a family firm. Dealing with family-run businesses and family-orientated companies. I'm sorry, you've always been a great worker, but we will have to let you go."

What more could I do? I leave his office, pack away my photos, lunch box and pens and head out of the office for the last time. I drive home completely numb with shock. When I park up outside our house I pick up my phone and notice a notification on the screen.

Mum, I'm going to Kirsty's, so don't panic. I'll be back about eight. We have an art project to work on. Her mum will text you to confirm it's okay. See you later.

Amy uses text speak with everyone else, but after me correcting her spelling and grammar on dozens of texts she just sticks to standard English these days with me. Sure enough there's a confirmation text from Claire. I reply with my thanks and offer to have Kirsty over to tea sometime soon.

I sigh heavily and climb out of the car and onto the pavement. My house might only be rented, but it's mine. I pay for it, all the bills, everything. And now I need to find another job, another way to support me and Amy. All the stability I've worked years for has crumbled away beneath me.

"Fuck you, Thunder," I mumble under my breath as I fit my key in the lock.

CHAPTER SIX

"What the—" I cry when I see the candles lit on the dining room table and the place settings for two. "Amy, I thought you were going to Kirsty's?"

"It's not Amy."

My jaw drops and my eyes widen when I see Thunder, dressed casually in jeans and a plain T-shirt walk through from the kitchen.

"How, I mean, why? I mean, what? I mean—what the holy fuck?"

"Yeah, I've got a lot of explaining to do. Sit down, Josie. I'll bring you a drink. Do you want tea?"

"Yeah, tea's good." I'm in a complete daze. I don't know what's going on and I can't work out how I feel, so I just go along with what's happening. A cup of tea is never a bad thing.

"Do you have milk and sugar?" Thunder calls from the kitchen.

"Milk, no sugar. I'm sweet enough," I answer on autopilot.

"You sure are," he responds with a sigh.

I bite down a scathing response and fight back the tears that accompany my boiling anger. If I'm so damn sweet, why did he use me so?

"Here you go, then." He carries the cup over and puts it on the corner of the coffee table.

"Thanks. Now I think you owe me one hell of an explanation."

"Sure, I know." He runs his fingers through his dark hair. "Okay, first of all, I'm incredibly sorry about all this. I want to make it right."

"Hmm." I tighten my lips and narrow my eyes. How much can I trust this man?

"Secondly, I didn't break in. Amy let me in."

"How in the hell? Have you been stalking my daughter?" Now a man can break my heart, but go near my daughter and I will pull his heart out and feed it to the urban foxes that howl in my garden on summer nights.

"No, no. I texted you yesterday but you never checked your phone. So I rang you and Amy answered. Wow, she's a really mature young lady, isn't she?"

I nod.

"Anyway, she told me how mad you were and stuff and well, together we came up with this plan to put things straight. She said it was best I cook for you. That always fixes things, apparently. Unfortunately I can't cook. So I thought we could order pizza—"

"Hang on a minute." I bang my hand down on my thigh. "Hang on, don't trivialise this. It's going to take a damn sight more than a fucking pizza to put this right."

"I know." He hangs his head, then looks up at me again. "But I really want to make it right."

"Okay then, pal. Tell me, what the fuck happened?"

"As much as I know is that my phone got misappropriated somewhere along the line. I had my phone all the time, but obviously someone got into it to access my data."

"Bollocks!"

"I know it sounds bad, but Josie, it's true. A whole load of stuff was taken off there. I've had to put a stop on my bank account because the data thief took a huge chunk of money out of it. Took my credit card for a whirl, too. I can show you, look. I've got a police crime number and everything."

I look down at the screen he's showing me and sure enough there's an email stating a crime number and the police's details and a list of all the data that Thunder claims has been stolen, including my image.

"Oh yeah." I shrug non-committedly.

"I think they sold the photo to a journo. If we can track down who was hanging around at the hotel, who could have got the regular pap photos, we might be able to track down the thief."

"Oh good," I snap. "Not like it's completely too late now anyway."

"I've issued takedown notices to anyone using that image. It's stolen property. I'm going to keep on top of it until every instance is taken down. I'll get it purged from search engines too. I will do all I can to have it erased. I'm so, so sorry, Josie." He puts his hand on my knee and I pull away sharply.

"No. It's not that easy. I lost my fucking job!"

"What?" he exclaims.

"Yeah, because of that image. Damage is done. I brought the company into ill repute, apparently. I have been let go. I am jobless. Jobless, Thunder."

The tears come. I don't want them to, but I can't hold them back. I am so angry, so sad, so confused. I'm feeling a million strong, negative emotions all at once, and the only way they can escape is through my eyes.

"Oh, fuck." Thunder sighs. I watch him reach a hand forward then snap it back before he touches me. "Jesus, Josie. I'm so sorry. I'll pay—"

"I don't want your fucking money! This isn't about money!"

"I know, Josie, I know, but you shouldn't be out of pocket just because of your association with me. I'll cover you until you get a new job. I know it won't be long. It's the least I can do. I insist."

"Fine," I growl, dashing the tears from my eyes with the back of my hands. "I really don't want to accept anything from you, but I have to pay the bills, keep a roof over our heads. I need to look after Amy." I gulp down more tears and my breath shudders out as I try to control my emotions. It's difficult when I think about my daughter and how much she depends on me.

"I know." His voice is soft, gentle. "I'll make sure you're both looked after."

"Thunder, don't."

"Don't what?"

"Pretend you care. That I'm more than a one-night stand to you. I know that's all it was."

"Oh, you do, do you?" There's steel in his tone now. He's not about placating me.

"Yes I do."

"Fuck, Josie. Would you listen to yourself! Judging me like that. I'm here doing my best for you. Do you think I'd do this if you were just some chick I picked up? I care about you, Josie, I really do."

"I wish I could believe that."

"I'm so sorry this happened. So very sorry. I understand you're feeling betrayed, angry, hurt. And I accept responsibility for that. I am so sorry. How can I make it better? I don't want to lose you from my life."

"Really?" I gulp, eyes stinging with tears.

"Really. We've got something special, and I'd kinda given up on ever finding that." Thunder cautiously puts his hand on my knee again. I don't knock it away this time.

"I've been so angry, Thunder. Not just because of the photos and the article, but because my dream was shattered. I thought we really had something. I mean, there was a definite connection between us, and then all this happened and it went away. I was left on my own again, picking up the pieces."

Thunder squeezes my knee, then wraps his arm around my shoulder. Again, I don't move to push him away.

"I didn't mean for you to get hurt. I was thinking of ways to see you again. It's not easy with us touring, but I was looking at gaps in my schedule and figuring out how I could get back to visit you. I was. Ask the guys. They were teasing me bad."

"Were they?"

"Yeah, bastards." He grins.

"Bastards." I agree. "I want to believe you, to believe all this. It's going to be hard."

"Yeah, I'm sure it will be, but I really want us to work this out. I'm going to do all I can to make things better. Please say you can begin to forgive me?"

I look into those green eyes, swirling with grey and brown patches. It's amazing how much eyes can change with mood. I can see nothing but sincerity and regret in them. "I can begin to try."

"That's all I can ask for, really." He holds me tighter and I relax into his arms. He kisses the top of my head. "Right then, shall I order that pizza?"

***

As we chew on our newly delivered pizza, we chat. The dining table is still set but we're sat on the sofa, the box propped between us.

"So how on earth are you here? I thought you were on tour?"

"We are, yeah. But no fucker wants to go to a concert on a Monday so Monday and Tuesday are usually our days off. The rest of the band are in Birmingham. Only I'm back here."

"Oh, right, you wanna stay here then? I can make this sofa pretty comfy."

"Nah, thanks for the offer. I'm booked in at a hotel. I didn't want to presume anything."

"Wise." I nod. "And anyway you'd not get a moment's peace from Amy asking all kinds of questions."

"Oh, I'm used to it." He laughs.

"No, I don't mean because of the band, I mean because you're dating me." I grin.

"So we're dating now?" He raises an eyebrow.

"Well, yeah. I guess. I think so, I mean, we are, aren't we?"

"Yes," he replies. "I was just teasing."

“Bastard,” I grumble. “Watch it, pal, I’ve only just started to forgive you.”

He pokes his tongue out playfully and we both laugh.

I know it’s not the most sensible thing in the world, this. I know I should be raging and cagey and not letting him anywhere near me. But God, how lonely and scary would that actually be? The most important thing is that I believe him and I want this to work, however crazy it is.

I can give him one more chance. What difference does it make? If it goes wrong it’ll break my heart, but if I can eke some more good from it first, why shouldn’t I? I trust this guy, for better or worse, and I’m not ready to give up on him yet.

***

When Amy gets in she squeals excitedly.

“It worked then.” She bounces.

I look up at Thunder from where I’m snuggled into his side.

“Yeah, it did,” he replies with a grin.

“Oh my God, I’m so happy for you!” She jumps round and round in a circle, waving her arms in the air.

"I should have a stern word with you, young lady. Answering my phone and conspiring with a strange man behind my back."

"But it's *Thunder*, Mum, God." She shakes her head. "I was sensible, Kirsty and her mum were with me the whole time while I let Thunder in. I didn't do it on my own. I'm not stupid."

"No, you're not, kid." I grin. "Thanks."

"You're welcome." She bumps down on the sofa on the other side of Thunder.

"So, can I get that autograph now?"

The rest of the evening passes in light-hearted conversation and wild fangirling from my child. I finally pry her away from Thunder and send her off to bed.

"See you tomorrow?" he asks as I see him out.

"Sure, I'll come over to the hotel after I drop Amy at the bus stop. I guess it'll be about nine o'clock."

"Okay, I'll be waiting for you." He kisses me, there, brazenly on my doorstep, and I kiss back with all the passion and joy that fills my heart.

CHAPTER SEVEN

Amy will not shut up about Thunder in the car while we drive towards her bus stop.

"You know not to talk to anyone at school about this, right?" I remind her yet again.

"I know, Mum. I'm only going to talk to Kirsty about it because she already knows. I'm not stupid."

"I know, love, I know. I just worry, that's all."

"Don't worry about me. I'm sensible. Thunder said so," she replies with much smugness.

"All right then, I'll see you later."

"See you, Mum. Have a good day."

"You too, hon, you too."

She knows I'm out of work, but is sure it'll all be all right because Thunder said so. I guess we're both hanging a lot on him. I should really be job hunting, not speeding across to his hotel wearing my second best knickers—the best are still drying on the radiator—because I'm expecting a morning of lustful shenanigans.

You only live once, though. I never thought I was the kind of person who would chase after storms but here I am, in hot pursuit of Thunder and the madness that a relationship with him will ensure.

I double check my phone as I rush into the reception of the far too posh for me hotel. It's not the one from last time—this one is far closer to me but part of the same chain.

648. I head to the lifts and towards his room, sending him a cheeky text warning of my imminent arrival. I stand in front of his door and pull in a deep breath. He opens it before I can even knock, grabs the front of my dress and drags me in, slamming the door shut with his other hand.

I want to yell at him for scaring me but his lips are on mine and his hands are roaming up and down my body and I'm completely incapable of any thought. I join in with equal passion, sliding my hands under his T-shirt, tracing over his soft belly and higher, to his harder muscles.

He pulls up on the edge of my dress and I allow him to completely remove it from my body, letting my hands fall to rest on his shoulders after they stood up in surrender in the air. The position made me think of that photo for a moment, but I don't let the negative associations linger. If I'm in for this, I've got to let that go.

"God, you're gorgeous," he groans, kissing my neck, nibbling and biting. His passionate assault pushes me back step by step until I'm up against the wall.

"As are you." I tug on his T-shirt and he retreats just enough so I can whip it off. His chest is covered in flames, a Chinese style dragon darts through them and I trace its journey down the middle of his body.

At the top of his jeans I stop and look up into his eyes. He nods gently, first slipping something out of the pocket and into his hand. I pop open the button and pull down the zip. He has no underwear beneath so all I see is him; hard, powerful flesh waiting for me. I drop to my knees before him, he moves to accommodate me and groans before I even lay my lips on his cock.

He is beautiful. His cock is red and straining, decorated with veins that I trace with my tongue. He tastes good, sweet and savoury, like the best kind of salted caramel. I'm lost in the need to please him, dipping my mouth around his cockhead, sliding my tongue down and exploring his length before bobbing my head up and down enthusiastically.

"Jesus," he groans, grabbing a handful of my hair. "Jesus, Josie."

I grin around his dick, relishing the way he fills out my mouth, the way he tastes, the way I have him completely at my mercy.

He jerks his hand back suddenly, dragging me off him with a pop and a gasp.

"I'll come if you do that anymore and right now I want to fuck you."

I'm not going to argue, so when he pulls on my hair again, I stand. He keeps the one hand wrapped in my hair, and holds me close to him with the other. Within seconds I'm once again pressed up against the wall. I am completely his, wanton and needy.

He lets go of me for a moment, opens the packet and slips the condom over himself. I wait for him to move back, to take me over to the bed or even the sofa but no, we don't move.

He kisses me again and this time his hands roam down my body, one seeking out the wetness of my pussy and God, I am soaked. He leisurely fucks his fingers into me for a while, making me moan and gasp against his lips, and filling the room with the scent of my sex.

I wonder what he's doing when he pulls my leg up to rest on his hip, then I feel his cock nudging at my entrance and I get it. He's going to fuck me up against the wall. I shudder with lust and apprehension. He pushes forward, using his free hand to lodge his cock against me.

"Fuck!" I exclaim. It feels so different him entering me this way. Once he is inside me a little way he grabs my other thigh.

My eyes flash wide with panic.

"Don't worry." He groans. "I've got you."

I nod and let him lift me, his cock shifting inside and lodge deeper within me.

"Oh God, oh God, oh God," I moan, wrapping my arms around his neck. He thrusts, banging me against the wall over and over. His pubis hits my clit and my orgasm rises. I gasp and groan. All I can do is hold on for the ride. I can't move. I just have to take it.

"Josie," he gasps. "Holy fuck, I love you."

"I love you too." It might be the heat of passion, it might be something true, something deep in our souls. I don't know, I don't care. I just revel in it.

"I love you." He drives each word into me with hard thrusts.

"Yes!" I exclaim, my pussy clenching around him and the rapture climbing to the point where I can't hold back any more. I flood him with my juices as I come.

"I love you!" He screams and pumps hard, filling me with his own climax seconds later, fuelling mine to higher heights of bliss.

He releases my thighs and my knees tremble as I have to hold my own weight up. He discards the condom and wraps me in his embrace again. I feel more grounded in his arms. Everything might not magically be okay, but this is right. This is how it should be. I know I need to be in Thunder's arms.

"Hey, if you're Thunder, does that make me lightning?" I ask.

He nods, I feel the top of his chin against my head. "Definitely. We're destined to be together."

It is completely crazy. I don’t know exactly where we’re going, but he’s right. We’re meant to be together, so I’m going to ride this storm to its very end.

ABOUT THE AUTHOR

Victoria Blisse is known as the Queen of Smut, Reverend to the kinky and is the Writer in Residence at Cocktails and Fuck Tales.

She's also an angel. Ask anyone.

Mancunian Odd Duck, her northern English quirkiness shows through in all of her stories along with her own particular brand of humour and romance that bring laughs and warm fuzzies in equal measure. Passion, love and laughter fill her works, just as they fill her busy life.

To find out more visit:

victoriablisse.co.uk

Printed in Great Britain
by Amazon

61482346R00054